Eerie
Elementary

The Art Show
ATTACKS!

By Jack Chabert
Illustrated by Matt Loveridge,
based on the art of Sam Ricks

BRANCHES
SCHOLASTIC INC.

READ ALL THE
Eerie Elementary
ADVENTURES!

TABLE OF CONTENTS

1: ART ATTACK...1

2: THE BLOB...7

3: SASH DASH!...11

4: THE SECRET IN THE DARK....................18

5: HIDDEN ROOM...22

6: FISTS OF DOOM!.....................................28

7: AN ORSON EERIE ORIGINAL.................34

8: THE SCHOOL . . . AND BEYOND!...........39

9: FREAKY FUND-RAISER...........................44

10: WHAT TO WEAR?..................................49

11: THE SHOW BEGINS 54

12: DOWN THE RIVER................................60

13: SOLD!..65

14: JURASSIC ART!.....................................73

15: TURN UP THE HEAT!...........................78

16: HUNG UP..86

For Evie Mandolese! — JC

Text copyright © 2018 by Max Brallier
Illustrations by Matt Loveridge copyright © 2018 by Scholastic Inc.

Library of Congress Cataloging-in-Publication Data

Names: Chabert, Jack, author. | Loveridge, Matt, illustrator. |
Chabert, Jack. Eerie Elementary ; 9.
Title: The art show attacks! / by Jack Chabert ; illustrated by Matt Loveridge.
Description: New York : Branches/Scholastic Inc., [2018] | Series: Eerie Elementary ; 9 | Summary: Sam is working on making a clay dinosaur for the school art show and sale when the clay suddenly comes to life and attacks him, a sure sign that once again Orson Eerie, whose spirit inhabits the school, is up to something—and it is up to Sam, Antonio, and Lucy to discover how a self-portrait of Orson figures into his evil plan.
Identifiers: LCCN 2018000609 | ISBN 9781338181975 (pbk : alk. paper) |
ISBN 9781338181982 (hardcover: alk. paper)
Subjects: LCSH: Haunted schools—Juvenile fiction. |
Art—Exhibitions—Juvenile fiction. | Self-portraits—Juvenile fiction. |
Elementary schools—Juvenile fiction. | Best friends—Juvenile fiction. |
Horror tales. | CYAC: Haunted places—Fiction. | Art—Fiction. |
Painting—Fiction. | Schools—Fiction. | Best friends—Fiction. |
Friendship—Fiction. | Horror stories. | LCGFT: Horror fiction.
Classification: LCC PZ7.C3313 Ar 2018 | DDC 813.6 [Fic]—dc23 LC record available at
https://lccn.loc.gov/2018000609

10 9 8 7 6 5 4 3 2 1   18 19 20 21 22

Printed in China 62
First edition, November 2018
Illustrated by Matt Loveridge
Edited by Katie Carella
Book design by Maria Mercado

"Lucy," Sam whispered. "What's that gunk you're working with?"

Lucy grinned. "This is called papier-mâché. I dip pieces of newspaper into a wet mix of water and flour. The paper turns goopy, and then it hardens as it dries. I'm making a bowl!"

"And I'm painting a picture of my dog, Rover," Antonio said.

Ms. Winter was checking on the students' work. She looked over at Sam's art project. "Remember, Sam," she said. "Clay stays soft at room temperature. It only hardens when heated. Lucy's project works the same way. You can dry it later this week."

Suddenly, there was a loud —

Sam jumped at the sound. But Lucy was just using a hair dryer to dry her papier-mâché bowl.

An instant later, Sam was startled for a *different* reason. He heard a bubbling sound, like a pot of boiling water.

Sam reached into his backpack to make sure his hall monitor sash was there. He wore it whenever he was on hall monitor duty.

At Eerie Elementary, the hall monitors were *different*. That's because Eerie Elementary was *different*. It was alive! It was a living, breathing thing that *fed* on students. And Sam, the hall monitor, was the school's protector.

Sam clutched the sash. He had a twisted feeling in his gut. Sam could sense things that other students couldn't. He could *feel* when something was wrong.

Whenever Sam had this feeling, Orson Eerie was behind it. Orson Eerie was the mad scientist who built Eerie Elementary almost one hundred years ago. Orson Eerie found a way to live forever — he *became* the school. He was Eerie Elementary. And Eerie Elementary was a monster . . .

Sam put his orange sash away just as the bubbling sound grew louder.

Sam gasped. His clay blob was moving!

He leaned in for a closer look. Then —

KER-SPLOOT!

The blob reached out and grabbed him! It yanked Sam's face **SMACK** down into the clay!

THE BLOB

Sam couldn't escape! His clay project had grabbed hold of his face! Sam whacked at the clay until —

POP!

He burst up from the blob, gasping for air.

Sam heard a few students laughing. "Did you fall *asleep* in your project?" their classmate Bryan asked.

Sam didn't know what to say. "I, um — uh —"

Lucy and Antonio looked at their friend. "Are you okay?" Antonio asked.

"Yes." Sam nodded. He wiped a clump of wet clay from his chin.

"What happened?" Lucy asked.

RING!

"Don't forget, class," Ms. Winter said as the students packed up their things. "The art show is *this Friday*! You *must* finish your projects by the end of the day on Thursday."

As Sam, Antonio, and Lucy walked out into the hall, Sam looked over his shoulder at the art room. He stopped . . .

One painting was *changing*. It had shown a beach sunset — but now it looked different. Sam rubbed his eyes. He could hardly believe it . . . Orson Eerie's face appeared on the painting!

A chill ran down Sam's spine. He tried to look away, but Orson Eerie's eyes were *staring* at him.

Lucy called from down the hall. "Come on, Sam! It's lunchtime!"

Sam felt like he had a golf ball stuck in his throat. He couldn't reply.

Finally, he was able to pull his eyes away from the painting. The last thing he saw was Orson Eerie's lips curl into a wicked smile.

SASH DASH!

Antonio munched on one of his famous peanut butter and jelly sandwiches. Lucy was opening her lunch bag as Sam plopped down beside his friends. Milk splashed when he set his tray down, but he barely noticed.

"Buddy, you still have clay in your hair!" Antonio said.

Lucy flicked off the glob. "Sam, what *really* happened in art class?"

Sam told them how the clay had *attacked* him. Lucy and Antonio were assistant hall monitors, so they were used to strange things happening at Eerie Elementary.

"At first, it felt like when my grandma kisses me," Sam explained. "She pulls me in and won't let go! But the clay was sticky and I couldn't breathe!"

"Wet grandma kisses are *the worst*!" Antonio said.

"And that's not all," Sam added. "One of the paintings on Ms. Winter's wall came to life! A sunset became Orson Eerie's face!"

Just then, Mr. Nekobi walked over. He had been mopping the floor nearby.

Mr. Nekobi was the old man who took care of Eerie Elementary. It was Mr. Nekobi who chose Sam to be a hall monitor. He had told Sam the truth about the school.

"Sam, did you really see a painting come alive?" Mr. Nekobi asked.

Sam nodded.

Mr. Nekobi leaned in and whispered, "Orson Eerie loved painting. He painted beautiful portraits and landscapes. He even helped paint the walls of this school."

Antonio shuddered. "Orson painted these walls?!"

"Yes," Mr. Nekobi said. "There's a little bit of Orson in almost every part of this school."

That gave everyone the chills.

Sam's forehead scrunched up. "Guys," he said. "I think we should take another look at Ms. Winter's classroom. I swear I saw Orson in one of those paintings."

"Let's do it," Lucy said. "We have a few minutes until lunch is over."

Antonio stood up. "Orson Eerie is up to something — and we've got to stop him!"

"Good luck," Mr. Nekobi said as he pushed his bucket toward the kitchen.

Sam threw on his hall monitor sash, and his friends followed him into the hall. But he stopped short.

"What is it?" Antonio asked.

"I'm not sure . . . ," Sam said. He looked down at his sash.

SWOOSH!

Sam was *yanked* forward.

"Whoa!" he exclaimed. The shiny sash was *tugging* him down the hallway. He pawed at locker doors, trying to slow down. "The sash is *pulling* me!"

"We're behind you, buddy!" Antonio yelled, running to catch up.

The sash pulled so hard, it jerked Sam off his feet. Sam's sneakers banged the steps as he was pulled up a staircase. Sam soared past the computer lab, and then the sash flung him down a hall.

He heard Lucy calling from below: "Sam! Where did you go?"

Sam shouted, "I'm upstairs! The fifth-grade hallway! Hurry!" Suddenly, Sam saw a brick wall in front of him. A dead end! Sam shut his eyes as —

BOOM!

"Ow!" Sam yelled.

He rubbed his nose and stepped back. The sash sagged. It had stopped pulling.

Sam was at the end of the fifth-grade hallway. The students were at lunch so the classroom doors were all shut. The hallway lights began to flicker and flash. Then —

The lights went out! Sam couldn't see *anything* but darkness.

THE SECRET IN THE DARK

4

Sam heard footsteps in the dark hallway. Lucy and Antonio had caught up.

"What was that?!" Antonio said, looking around as his eyes adjusted to the dark.

An icy chill came down the hall. The friends huddled together.

"Some strange force *pulled* on my sash. It *whipped* me down the hallway," Sam explained. "It let go of me here. Then the lights went out."

He touched the wall in front of him. The bricks felt cold and damp.

"Wait a second," Lucy said. "What is that green stuff?"

Neon goo started oozing through the cracks in the wall. It was the color of a highlighter. It dripped between the bricks.

Sam poked it. He rubbed his fingers together. "It's paint."

"Strange," Antonio said. He gently pressed one of the bricks, and it moved!

"Whoa!" Lucy exclaimed. She pushed a brick, too.

Then Antonio pushed another one, and a gurgling sound came from the wall —

BLUB. BLUB. BLUB.

Wet paint dripped onto the friends' shoes.

"Guys, what's happening?" Lucy asked.

The three friends stepped back as the bricks began to move and slide on their own. It was like a giant, real-life Jenga game!

Soon, there was a large opening in the wall.

"This looks like the entrance to a cave," Sam said.

They peered inside. There was something beyond the wall — but it was too dark to see *what*.

Suddenly, the sash *yanked* Sam forward. "Yikes!" Sam cried.

Antonio grabbed his friend's shirt. "I have you, Sam!"

"And I've got *you*, Antonio!" Lucy said.

But the sash yanked again — and the friends tumbled *through* the opening. They landed on a cold floor in a small, dark room. They could barely see.

"I have a feeling we should *not* be in here," whispered Antonio.

Lucy dusted herself off. "I agree."

Sam felt along the wall until he found a light switch. The instant he flicked it on, Antonio screamed, "GHOST!"

HIDDEN ROOM

5

"That is definitely *not* a ghost," Sam said to his friends.

Lucy laughed. "It's just a big white sheet!" she exclaimed.

"Whoops. False alarm," Antonio said. "But this room *is* scary."

Sam walked to the center of the small room. The sheet hung over an artist's easel. It was splattered with paint.

Sam lifted one corner of the sheet. The friends gasped.

Orson Eerie's eyes stared out at them from the canvas.

"Someone painted a portrait of Orson!" Antonio said.

"Not just *someone*," Lucy said. "Look!" She lifted a painter's smock off a dusty coatrack.

The letters *O.E.* were stitched onto the smock.

"Those are Orson's initials!" Sam exclaimed.

"This must have been Orson's secret art studio!" Lucy said.

Antonio stepped away from the painting. "That means this is a self-portrait," he said. "A painting Orson did *of himself*."

RING!

Lunch was over. "We should get back," Antonio said.

Sam turned to leave, but —

THUD!

He bumped into the wall.

Lucy took a step backward. "The opening is gone! It's a regular brick wall again!"

Sam felt for a place to push and open the wall. But there were no more wiggly, moving bricks. The goo was gone, too.

"Hey! Antonio, cut it out!" Lucy exclaimed.

Antonio looked confused. "What did I do?!"

Lucy replied, "I *know* you were pulling my backpack."

Just then, Sam shouted, "Antonio's not pulling you! ORSON'S PAINTING IS! IT'S ALIVE!"

Antonio and Lucy whirled around. Two strange, paint-covered hands reached out from the Orson Eerie portrait! One had hold of Lucy's backpack strap.

CRASH!

The hand *yanked* Lucy's backpack off her shoulder and *hurled* it onto the floor.

"Watch out, guys!" Sam shouted. He leapt back as the hand swatted at him. Lucy ducked as the other hand swiped at her.

The hands turned to fists, and —

SMASH! CRUNCH!

The fists pounded the floor!

"Orson's fists are going to smash us to bits!" screamed Antonio.

Sam's eyes darted around the room. He saw no way out. He saw no escape at all!

FISTS OF DOOM!

Orson Eerie's self-portrait was *alive*. Two painted fists pounded the floor!

Sam spotted dusty old art tools scattered across a wooden desk.

Those long brushes could be used like swords, he thought. *And those wooden palettes are like shields. Even if we can't escape this room, we need to defeat these fists!*

"Catch!" Sam yelled, tossing tools to his friends. "It's time to fight back!"

Antonio swung a long brush through the air like a ninja with a sword! But —

WHACK!

One fist smacked the brush away! Antonio lifted the wooden palette — and just in time! The fist *punched* his shield. Antonio staggered across the room and fell to the floor.

"I'm not letting giant paint fists bash my friends!" Lucy shouted. She jabbed her brush and swung her shield. But Orson Eerie's fists opened into wide hands! They *snatched* the brush and palette away! A moment later —

CRUNCH!

The fists crushed Lucy's sword and shield. Splinters of wood shot across the floor.

"This isn't working!" Antonio called out.

Sam found more art supplies on shelves above the desk. "Lucy! Maybe something here can help us!"

Orson Eerie's fists pounded the ground. The floor quaked with each hit.

"The floor is like a trampoline!" Antonio yelled as he tried to stand. "Trampolines are usually the best — but not this one! Hurry, guys!"

Sam and Lucy quickly looked through the shelves of art supplies.

"PAINT THINNER!" Lucy exclaimed, grabbing a huge can.

"Watch out!" Antonio shouted across the room. "Behind you!"

Two massive hands reached for Sam and Lucy. Lucy yanked off the can's lid, and —
SPLOOSH!

Sam and Lucy hurled the paint thinner into the air! The stinky liquid rained down on the monstrous fists. Orson Eerie's portrait trembled on the canvas.

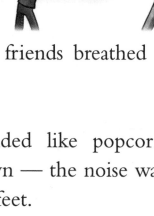

POOF!

The hands evaporated into thin air. Gone! The friends breathed a sigh of relief.

But then —

SNAP! POP! It sounded like popcorn popping. Sam looked down — the noise was coming from beneath his feet.

"The floor is splitting in half!" Lucy said.

"Orson's superstrong fists broke the floor!" Antonio exclaimed.

A crack zigzagged between the friends. Light shined up from below.

KA-KRAK!

The floor split wide open! The friends tumbled *through* the floor, and *through* the ceiling below!

The friends all screamed.

AHHHHHHHH!

AN ORSON EERIE ORIGINAL

$\mathbf{S}$am, Lucy, and Antonio landed with a
THUD! They were sprawled out on a desk.
Bits of ceiling sprinkled down on them.

Sam sat up. Their art teacher, Ms. Winter,
had her hand over her mouth.

"Um, hello, Ms. Winter," said Sam as he
shook dirt from his hair.

The hall monitors glanced around. They had fallen through the floor of Orson Eerie's old art studio — and dropped right into Ms. Winter's art class. Twenty-two shocked fourth-graders stared at them.

Suddenly, there was a crashing sound from above.

"Watch out!" Lucy said.

The friends covered their heads.

Orson Eerie's self-portrait toppled onto the hall monitors!

Ms. Winter swooped over. She didn't seem to mind the mess. She was smiling from ear to ear!

"Oh my! This is an exciting discovery!" Ms. Winter squealed as she picked up the painting. "Do you know what this is?"

"Ah . . . art?" Antonio asked.

"Not just *any* art . . . It's an Orson Eerie original!" Ms. Winter exclaimed. "And I know *exactly* what to do with it!"

Sam, Lucy, and Antonio stood up.

Ms. Winter, still smiling, announced, "This painting will be the *highest-priced piece of art* at Friday's art show! For one hundred dollars, someone will get to take *this treasure* home!"

She held the painting above her head like a trophy. Sam, Lucy, and Antonio were stunned. The fourth-graders looked confused, too.

"Let's get out of here!" Lucy whispered, motioning to her friends.

The hall monitors quietly escaped into the hall as Ms. Winter placed the painting on an easel by her desk. The evil painting had a new home.

THE SCHOOL . . . AND BEYOND!

Sam, Lucy, and Antonio snuck into Ms. Grinker's classroom. Luckily, she didn't notice they were late. They did their best to focus on schoolwork for the rest of the afternoon. Finally, the school day was over.

"This was a superweird day," Sam said as they hurried across the playground. The friends were eager to get home.

"You know what this all means, right?" Lucy asked.

Sam was pretty sure he was thinking the same thing Lucy was. He pulled his friends into a huddle.

"I think Orson Eerie *wanted* us to discover that old art studio," Sam said. "He pulled my sash — and broke that floor — so we would find his painting!"

"But why?" Antonio asked. "What is so important about a painting?"

"Good question," Sam said.

"Wait!" Lucy exclaimed. "Remember when the school was almost torn down? Remember Orson's drawing with the arrows on it?"

Sam recalled the drawing — it proved that Orson Eerie's powers could leave the school. The thought of Orson Eerie's creepy powers spreading *outside* of Eerie Elementary was horrible.

"Right!" Sam said. "Someone will buy the painting at the art show! They'll take it home! Orson's power will *spread beyond the school grounds.*"

Antonio nodded. "As hall monitors, I bet we can only battle him on school grounds! This is awful! If someone buys that painting, Orson's evil could spread *anywhere*."

"Or *everywhere*," Lucy whispered.

The friends shuddered.

"There's only one way to stop Orson," Sam said. "*We* need to buy that painting on Friday."

"I agree," Lucy said. "We *cannot* let that painting leave school grounds."

"But Ms. Winter said it's going to cost one hundred dollars," Antonio said, frowning. "How much money do we have?"

The friends turned their pockets inside out. Lint fell from Lucy's pocket. Antonio had the crusts of his peanut butter and jelly sandwich.

Sam sighed. "I only have my hall monitor sash. That won't help us now."

Lucy's face lit up. "THAT'S IT!" she exclaimed. She pointed to Sam's sash. "Art is being sold to raise money for the school, right? So, we will just have to raise money for ourselves!"

Sam and Antonio had no idea what Lucy was talking about.

She grinned. "Trust me! Sam, bring a big glass jar to school tomorrow. My plan will make sense then." Lucy ran home. "I have to get started!"

Sam wondered, *What is Lucy planning? And will it be enough to stop Orson Eerie?*

FREAKY FUND-RAISER

It was Tuesday morning. Sam and Antonio sat against their lockers. They rolled the empty glass jar back and forth.

Seconds later, Lucy arrived carrying a poster board. And she was wearing a big hat with flowers on it.

"Um, nice hat . . . ," Sam said. "I think? Actually, what's with the hat, Lucy?"

Everyone was working on their projects for the show.

Ms.Winter's room was set up differently from other classrooms. The students' desks formed a giant circle around Ms. Winter's desk. Her favorite student artwork hung on the wall.

ART ATTACK

"Hey! Quit it!" Sam Graves said. His friend Antonio was poking at a clay blob on Sam's desk. Sam was trying, and failing, to mold the clay into a dinosaur.

Ms. Winter, the art teacher, looked up. "Class, *please* take this project seriously," she said. "Your art will be sold at Friday's Eerie Elementary Art Show to raise money for new art supplies."

The paint had been a raging river — and then it was a trickling stream — and then it was nothing at all. Sam cradled the jar.

"We've got to get to the auditorium!" Lucy said.

They jumped to their feet and sped down the halls. They were out of breath when they finally burst through the auditorium doors.

Sam saw Ms. Winter holding Orson Eerie's self-portrait. She asked, "Which lucky buyer will go home with this?"

"We will!" Sam shouted. "We have one hundred dollars to buy the painting!"

The audience gasped.

"SOLD!" Ms. Winter announced. "This painting now belongs to our hall monitors, Sam, Lucy, and Antonio! It's wonderful seeing our students' love of art!"

Sam, Lucy, and Antonio hurried toward the stage. Change rattled as they climbed the steps.

"How will you three decide whose house to hang the painting in?" Ms. Winter asked.

"We're going to keep it at school," Sam said. "So everyone can see and enjoy it."

Once they gave Ms. Winter the money jar, the painting would be theirs.

As Sam held out the jar, a scream came from the audience! Then another! And another!

Everyone was jumping up and pointing at the floor.

"What's happening?!" Ms. Winter cried.

Sam saw wet clay oozing up *everywhere*. It pushed through cracks in the floorboards.

Just then, Sam spotted his clay dinosaur sculpture near them on the stage. It looked wet again, and it looked like it was melting! It was seeping through the stage — and at the same time, clay was rising up through the auditorium floor!

Sam glanced at Mr. Nekobi. The old man understood that the hall monitors needed help. He hurried onto the stage. "Nothing to be concerned about!" he told the crowd. "The recent construction work done to the school probably turned up some mud. Let's calmly head outside while our hall monitors get this cleaned up."

Everyone left the auditorium. And just in time!

As soon as the doors shut, the hall monitors saw Sam's art project. His clay dinosaur had completely risen from the floor.

Lucy gasped. "Sam — your dinosaur! *It's a T. rex*!?"

"You *had* to make a T. rex, huh, Sam!?" Antonio asked.

Sam shrugged. "It's always been my favorite dinosaur . . . that is, until now!"

The T. rex was as big as the real thing! Its giant jaws chomped as the dinosaur stomped toward the hall monitors.

JURASSIC ART!

14

"There is a monstrous clay T. rex in the middle of our auditorium!" Sam cried out.

"Orson must be mad his painting won't be leaving school grounds after all!" Lucy said.

The T. rex's tail snapped in the air. Its tiny clay eyes looked right at Sam.

GRRRRAAAWR!

The monster roared.

"It wants the jar!" Sam said. "It knows if we lose this money, we can't buy the painting!"

"Well then, hold on to that jar!" Antonio cried. "RUN!"

Sam dashed beneath the monster's swinging tail. He cradled the jar like a star running back carries a football! *This Orson Eerie dino monster will never catch me!* he thought.

But Sam was wrong.

CRASH!

He tripped over an auditorium seat, and the glass jar smashed against the floor. Coins scattered around the auditorium.

The giant clay T. rex stomped toward the broken jar! Dollar bills became stuck to the bottom of its wet clay feet! Its swinging tail gathered up coins!

"OUR MONEY!" yelled Sam.

"Watch out!" Lucy cried. The three friends ducked as the T. rex's tail slapped against the floor. **SMACK!**

Its tail *whipped* the change toward them. Nickels and quarters pounded the wall.

Sam, Antonio, and Lucy all scrambled to get away.

"Never run in a straight line!" Antonio yelled. "I learned that from watching action movies!"

They zigzagged between chairs.

The T. rex's tail swung again. More coins were hurled through the air.

KRAK! Quarters smacked into Antonio's shoulder. "Ouch!" he exclaimed. "Keep your heads down, guys!"

Sweat poured off the friends as they dodged and dived around the flying coins. "I'm baking in these footie pajamas!" Lucy said.

Suddenly, Sam had an idea. "Clay needs to be *heated up* to harden!" he called out.

GRRRRAAAWR!

"Yeah! So?" Lucy yelled over the T. rex's monstrous roar.

Antonio just barely dodged a flying nickel. "Lucy! Think about it: If clay gets hot enough, it dries out!" he exclaimed. "It turns stiff, like stone!"

Lucy's eyes lit up. "So we need some heat!"

Sam ducked flying nickels and dimes. He yelled, "Follow me!"

TURN UP THE HEAT!

Sam, Lucy, and Antonio raced out of the auditorium. They ran through the halls to the art room.

"Grab as many hair dryers as you can and plug them in!" Sam shouted.

"There are a bunch near the papier-mâché materials!" Lucy shouted as they ran.

CLOMP! SQUISH! SQUASH! The T. rex's heavy clay feet squashed the floor behind them. The dinosaur's sharp fangs nipped at their backs.

Antonio grabbed the water fountain for balance as he slid around a corner. "Woo-hoo!" he yelled. "Our footie pj's are making us faster than ever!"

After speeding and sliding down the hallway, the friends burst into Ms. Winter's art room.

"Over here!" Lucy shouted.

Behind them, the T. rex squeezed through the doorway. When it lifted its head, bits of clay streaked the ceiling.

"Catch!" Lucy said. She tossed hair dryers to Sam and Antonio.

"Six?!" Antonio exclaimed.

"We need *a lot* of heat!" Lucy said.

They jammed the plugs into the wall and cranked up the knobs on the hair dryers.

"TIME TO HEAT THINGS UP!" Sam shouted.

Sam, Lucy, and Antonio pointed their hair dryers at the T. rex. The dinosaur snapped its jaws as it stomped toward them. The hair dryers rumbled in the hall monitors' hands. They blasted the T. rex with hot air.

The T. rex was slowing. Its legs and tail were hardening.

But its huge mouth still roared, and its teeth still snapped!

"The T. rex is too tall for us to reach all of it! Our hair dryers are only hitting its bottom half!" yelled Sam. "We have to get higher . . ."

Antonio looked up. The hole in the ceiling was still there. "We can climb up into Orson Eerie's old art room!" he shouted.

"Perfect!" Lucy said.

The hall monitors scrambled up onto Ms. Winter's desk. Together, they pulled themselves through the crumbled ceiling. They made it just in time!

CHOMP!

"The T. rex nearly got me!" Antonio said.

"Plug back in!" Lucy cried. The friends quickly powered up the hair dryers.

VROOM!

Sam and his friends blasted the T. rex from above!

The dinosaur started quaking and shaking! The clay was hardening. It was turning to stone!

"It's working!" Lucy yelled.

"Of course it is! It was *my* idea!" Antonio shouted over the whirring hair dryers.

They kept blowing hot air into the T. rex's face. Its head whipped back. It wailed.

HOOOOOWWWWLLLLL!!!

Then —
SMASH!
The dinosaur fell over! It hit the ground so
hard that it broke into a thousand little pieces!
And as it did, Sam saw something . . .
The face of Orson Eerie.

He saw it in the cracking bits of hardened clay. Sam saw Orson Eerie's lips curl into the same wicked smile he had seen before.

But then the smile was gone.

The rock-hard clay had shattered completely. The Orson Eerie T. rex was no more.

The hall monitors climbed down from the ceiling and slumped on the floor.

A moment later, the sound of rushing feet and nervous voices came from out in front of the school.

"We still need to pay for the painting," Sam said. "Come on!"

HUNG UP

Sam, Lucy, and Antonio burst into the auditorium.

"Look!" Antonio said.

Parents, teachers, and students hurried back inside.

Ms. Winter stepped onto the stage and scooped up Orson Eerie's painting. "Phew!" she said. "It's still in fine condition!"

"Ms. Winter! We have the money!" Sam called out, running up onstage.

"But it's, uh . . . everywhere . . . ," Antonio added.

Dollar bills and loose change were scattered across the floor. It was going to take a *long* time to gather it up.

Thankfully, Mr. Nekobi said, "I'm certain our hall monitors have one hundred dollars. I counted it yesterday. I will help them collect it all tonight."

"We will get every last penny," Lucy said. "Promise!"

"Well then," Ms. Winter said. "Sam, Antonio, and Lucy, congratulations! This painting is yours!"

Sam grabbed the painting. The sooner this was over, the better.

"Everyone, thank you for coming to our art show," Ms. Winter said, "and thank you for helping Eerie Elementary get new art supplies for its students!"

The crowd made its way outside.

Mr. Nekobi said, "Let's hang the painting now."

The hall monitors hurried into the hallway. Sam handed over the painting. Mr. Nekobi held it up on the wall near the front entrance.

"A little to the left," Sam said.

"A bit higher," Lucy added.

"No, lower," Antonio suggested.

At last, Mr. Nekobi hung it and stepped back. They all agreed it looked good.

But then Sam realized something: "We hung this creepy painting right across from Eerie Elementary's front doors!" he exclaimed.

"We can't miss it," Lucy said.

"We'll have to look at his awful face every single day," Antonio groaned.

Yes, Sam thought. *Every single day.*

And worst of all — Sam knew this face would be looking at them, too. Orson Eerie's pale, painted eyes would always be watching them . . .

Shhhh!

This news is top secret: **Jack Chabert** is a pen name for *New York Times*–bestselling author Max Brallier. (Max uses a made-up name instead of his real name so Orson Eerie won't come after him, too!)

Max was once a hall monitor at Joshua Eaton Elementary School in Reading, MA. But today, Max lives in a super-weird old apartment building in New York City. His days are spent writing, playing video games, and reading comic books. And at night, he walks the halls, always prepared for the moment when his building will come alive.

Max is the author of more than twenty books for children, including the middle-grade series The Last Kids on Earth and Galactic Hot Dogs. Visit the author at www.MaxBrallier.com.

Matt Loveridge loves illustrating children's books. When he's not painting or drawing, he likes hiking, biking, and drinking milk from the carton. He lives in the mountains of Utah with his wife and kids, and their black dog named Blue.

How Much Do You Know About

Eerie Elementary

The Art Show ATTACKS?

What is in the secret room Sam and his friends find at the end of the fifth-grade hallway?

Reread page 24. What is a *self-portrait*? How is this different from a *portrait*?

Why don't Sam, Lucy, and Antonio want Orson Eerie's painting to leave the school? Reread page 41 for clues.

Sam, Lucy, and Antonio need to raise money fast. Lucy has the idea to fund-raise. Has there ever been a fund-raiser at your school? Explain.

Lucy makes her art project out of papier-mâché. Papier-mâché is made of three ingredients: water, flour, and newspaper. Research how to make papier-mâché, and create your own craft!

Lucy smiled and turned the poster board around.

Sam and Antonio didn't understand.

Lucy groaned. "It's simple! We need one hundred dollars. So we're going to have our own fund-raiser to raise the money!"

STUDENTS, TEACHERS! WHILE MS. WINTER DRESSES UP THE HALLS WITH ART, YOU CAN DRESS UP YOUR HALL MONITORS! $1 per entry!

"But what are we *selling*?" Sam asked.

"We're selling our outfits!" Lucy said.

"No way!" Antonio exclaimed. "I like these pants!"

"Not the outfits we're *wearing*," Lucy said, laughing. "Listen. Every student or teacher who puts one dollar in the jar gets to write down a silly costume idea. They drop their entry into this hat. Once we reach our goal of one hundred dollars, Mr. Nekobi will pick *one* silly costume entry from the hat. That's what we wear on Friday!"

Suddenly, Ms. Winter walked by. She spotted the sign and said, "What a clever idea! So creative!"

Sam instantly stopped thinking about Lucy's fund-raising plan. He saw that Ms. Winter was carrying something large, wrapped in brown paper.

Sam realized what it was. A corner of the paper had come undone . . .

It was Orson Eerie's painting. And Orson Eerie was *staring* at Sam! He seemed to be watching Sam's every move.

Ms. Winter turned the corner, and the hall monitors set up their fund-raising table. They had their jar, their sign, and Lucy's wacky hat. And they only had three days to raise one hundred dollars — Tuesday, Wednesday, and Thursday.

Their classmates and other students loved their fund-raiser! They tried to outdo one another with ridiculous costume ideas. Even Principal Winik paid a dollar to join in on the fun. He wanted the hall monitors to dress up as clowns! Sam *really* hoped Mr. Winik's entry wouldn't be picked.

STUDENTS, TEACHERS!
WHILE MS. WINTER DRESSES UP THE HALLS WITH ART, YOU CAN DRESS UP YOUR HALL MONITORS!
$1 per entry!

At the end of the day on Wednesday, Lucy counted the money from the jar. There were stacks of coins in front of her. "We've almost hit our goal," she said. "We have eighty-two dollars."

Just then, Ms. Winter's voice came over the loudspeaker. "Students, a reminder! Tomorrow is your *last day* to finish your art projects. All students must have a finished piece for the art show!"

Oh no! I've been so busy raising money for Orson's painting, I totally forgot about my project, Sam thought. *I have to get to work!*

WHAT TO WEAR?

Sam was drying his clay dinosaur. It was Thursday morning. The first bell hadn't rung yet, but Sam had already been in the art room for an hour.

Ms. Winter was rushing around, preparing for the show. She kept taking student artwork from the room and hanging it in the hallways.

Sam felt like each piece she carried out — drawings and paintings and doodles — was *watching* him.

Sam shook his head. He needed to focus on finishing his project. He was close.

He looked down at his clay dinosaur. And he gulped. Sam felt like the dinosaur's eyes were watching him, too . . .

Sam felt like *everything* was watching him.

"WE HAVE HIT OUR GOAL! One hundred dollars!"

Sam was jolted out of his daze. He looked up and saw Lucy happily marching into the art room. Antonio followed. He was carrying their money jar over his head.

"We just gave Mr. Nekobi our hat full of ideas so he can pick the winning entry," Antonio said.

"And I've just finished my project!" Sam said, shutting off his hair dryer.

"You were still working on it?" Lucy asked.

"Lucy and I finished our projects *days ago*," Antonio teased.

Sam rolled his eyes as he set his dinosaur on Ms. Winter's desk.

Then Sam and his friends hurried to Ms. Grinker's classroom.

It was a *long* day. The hall monitors knew that at any moment, Mr. Nekobi could come over the loudspeaker. He would announce the winning costume, which could be anything!

KRR-CHH!

Everyone looked up at the loudspeaker.

Ms. Winter's voice filled the room: "Happy Thursday, students! Don't forget the art show is tomorrow. And now, Mr. Nekobi has a fun announcement!"

Sam looked at his friends. Mr. Nekobi was about to reveal the winning costume.

"This is the big moment," Antonio said under his breath. "I *really* hope we get to dress up as something cool, like superheroes! Or life-size peanut butter and jelly sandwiches!"

Finally, Mr. Nekobi read the winning entry aloud. They would *not* be wearing awesome costumes. Not even close . . .

THE SHOW BEGINS . . .

11

"**Y**ou three look *real* comfy!" Bryan shouted from the swing set.

It was Friday morning. Sam, Antonio, and Lucy were walking across the playground. All their classmates were laughing.

Sam's cheeks turned red. "We look like babies," he groaned. The money jar was in Sam's backpack. With each shuffle of Sam's toasty feet, change rattled.

"Forget about them," Lucy said. "All that matters is my idea worked! We have enough money to buy Orson's painting tonight."

"But why did Mr. Nekobi choose *footie pajamas* from the hat? This is so embarrassing!" Antonio complained.

All morning, Sam heard their classmates laughing. It went on through lunch and recess. At the end of the day, their classmates were *still* laughing. It wasn't just because the friends *looked* silly — they also kept slipping and sliding down the halls. The footie pj's didn't have rubber soles!

Finally, the Eerie Elementary Art Show was beginning! Parents, neighbors, and other townspeople poured into the school. They looked at the artwork lining the halls. Sam heard lots of *oohing* and *ahhing*.

Soon, everyone entered the auditorium and found seats. Ms. Winter stepped onstage. She would show off each piece of art. Then, the person who wanted to buy the piece would come forward and pay for it.

Sam, Antonio, and Lucy watched from the hallway. Sam saw his own project onstage: his clay dinosaur.

The three friends were about to enter the very full auditorium when Sam saw one of the drawings on the wall *move*!

Antonio and Lucy gasped. They saw it, too: a stick-figure drawing was coming to life!

Sam quickly closed the auditorium doors.

They could not believe what they were seeing. The stick figure slowly peeled itself off the paper. It landed on the floor and began trotting toward them.

"It has bendy arms like spaghetti . . . ," Sam said softly.

"And its arms are growing!" Lucy said.

The friends all watched, scared, until —

YANK!

The figure's long arms reached out and *plucked* the money jar from Sam's backpack.

The friends were too stunned to move.

Suddenly, all the paintings started coming to life! And the jar was being tossed back and forth down the hall — away from Sam and his friends!

"Orson Eerie is making the artwork play keep-away!" Sam said as a drawing of a spider caught the jar in its fuzzy legs.

"It's like when we play that game monkey-in-the-middle at recess!" Lucy exclaimed.

Antonio raced down the hall. He shouted, "HEY! GIVE US BACK OUR JAR!"

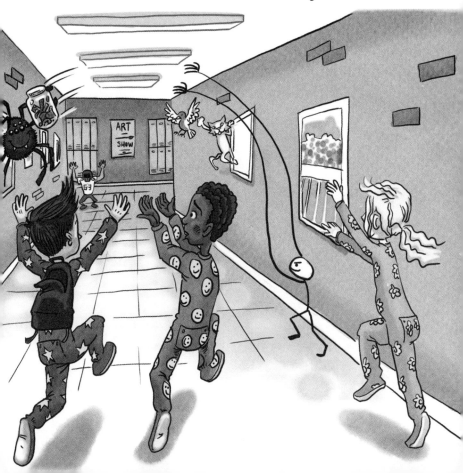

DOWN THE RIVER

Sam, Lucy, and Antonio chased the money jar as artwork hurled it back and forth down the hall.

Sam reached for it, but it flew over his head.

"This way!" Lucy yelled. She sped around a corner.

A painting of a tree *flung* the jar up a flight of stairs. It was caught by a doodle of an elderly woman. The woman threw the jar to a sketch of a caterpillar.

The hall monitors raced up the steps — then stopped.

Sam whispered, "Do you hear something *dripping*?"

"More than dripping," Lucy said.

Antonio said, "That sounds like a gushing faucet."

Sam gasped. Paint was dripping from every single piece of art! It ran down the walls and puddled on the floor. The canvases on the wall were drained of color — they all turned white! There was *so much* paint, it began rising like a river!

All of a sudden —

A river of paint rushed toward them.

"Ahh!" Lucy cried out as the friends were swept up in a flood of thick, wet, multicolored paint.

"Look!" Sam said. "The jar is over there!"

It was bobbing in the river of paint. Every time the friends got close to it, the jar was carried farther away.

"Quick, hold hands!" Antonio shouted. "If we form a chain, we can reach it!"

Antonio grabbed Lucy's hand. Lucy gripped Sam's. Sam tried to grab the jar . . .

"I can't quite get it!" Sam yelled.

They heard Ms. Winter's voice coming from inside the auditorium: "Now for sale: Our most prized piece! A self-portrait painted by Orson Eerie!"

"Hurry! We are almost out of time!" Lucy shouted.

The paint river flung them around a corner.

Sam's fingertips scraped the jar. "So . . . close . . . " He felt his heart pounding as he lunged for the jar!

"**G**OT IT!" Sam exclaimed as he finally grasped the money jar.

The instant Sam had the jar in his hands, the rushing river of paint began to dry up.

"The paint's starting to separate!" Antonio shouted.

Globs of paint leapt up onto the wall and back into their paintings. Blank canvases were full of color again!

The hall monitors bumped across the dry floor and bounced to a stop.